MATCHBOX HERO·CITY

EMERGENCY!
Storytime Collection

BY ANNIE AUERBACH
ILLUSTRATED BY S.I. INTERNATIONAL
& ARTFUL DOODLERS

LITTLE SIMON
New York   London   Toronto   Sydney

LITTLE SIMON

An imprint of Simon & Schuster Children's Publishing Division

1230 Avenue of the Americas, New York, New York 10020

Police on Patrol and *Three-Alarm Fire!* copyright © 2003 by Mattel, Inc.

Building Heroes and *Emergency!* copyright © 2004 by Mattel, Inc.

Copyright © 2006 by Mattel, Inc. MATCHBOX and associated trademarks

and trade dress are owned by and used under license from Mattel, Inc.

All rights reserved, including the right of reproduction in whole or in part in any form.

LITTLE SIMON is a registered trademark of Simon & Schuster, Inc.,

and associated colophon is a trademark of Simon & Schuster, Inc.

Manufactured in the United States of America

First Edition

2 4 6 8 10 9 7 5 3 1

ISBN-13: 978-1-4169-1860-8

ISBN-10: 1-4169-1860-4

These titles were previously published individually by Little Simon.

CONTENTS

POLICE
on Patrol

By Annie Auerbach

Illustrated by Jesus Redondo and Ivan & Moxo

Early Monday morning a group of officers assembled in the Hero City police station for roll call.

"Settle down, everyone," said the police lieutenant. "I know you're anxious to hit the streets and start your shift."

The lieutenant updated the officers on things they should watch out for on their patrols. "That's it for now. Be safe."

Officer Matt Sheldon and his partner, Officer Barbara Torres, headed to their patrol car. They worked together patrolling the same beat—beat number sixteen. They made a great team.

"Shall I drive?" asked Officer Sheldon.

Officer Torres laughed. "Every day you try that. No way! Now get in and buckle up!"

Suddenly a call came through from the dispatcher. "One Adam-sixteen. Code two."
Officer Sheldon picked up the hand radio and said, "Sixteen. Go ahead."

"We have a huge traffic pileup at the intersection of First and Hill," continued the dispatcher.

"Copy," replied Officer Sheldon. "We're on our way."

Officer Torres turned on the red-and-blue flashing lights. The siren wailed as she floored the gas pedal. She expertly weaved in and out of traffic, safely and carefully.

"You're the best driver on the street," Matt said to his partner.

"I know," Barbara replied with a chuckle. "I *love* driving this police car!"

Before long the officers arrived at the scene. A truck had crashed. There were piles of stinky fish everywhere!

No one seemed to be hurt, so Officer Torres asked, "What exactly happened?"

"A dog ran right in front of my car," a woman replied. "I swerved so I wouldn't hit the poor little fella and—"

"And you plowed right into me!" a truck driver interrupted.

"Calm down. Calm down," Officer Torres told them.

Meanwhile Officer Sheldon began to direct traffic. He directed traffic with one hand and held his nose with the other!

Eventually tow trucks were called in. By lunchtime a cleanup crew had arrived to pick up the stinky fish.

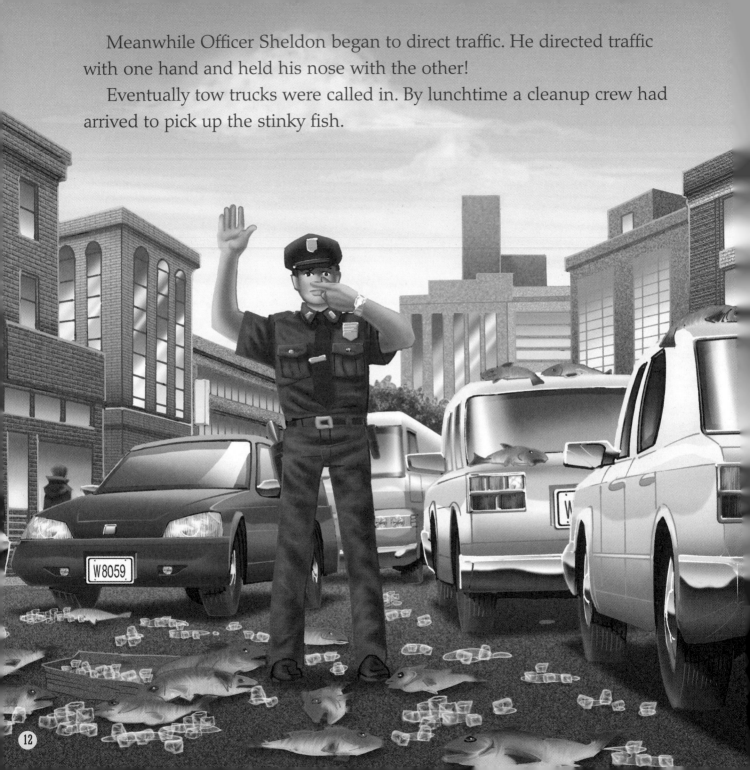

Back in the patrol car Officer Torres joked, "Let's not have fish for lunch!"
"I agree!" said Officer Sheldon with a laugh.

After lunch the officers patrolled the neighborhood.

Another call came in around 1:35 P.M. "One Adam-sixteen. Code three."

"Sixteen. Go ahead," Officer Sheldon responded.

"Four fifty-nine in progress. Burglary at Hero City Bank," said the dispatcher.

"Copy. We're en route," said Officer Sheldon.

With the lights flashing and siren blaring, the patrol car sped through the streets. It was the police to the rescue!

The officers arrived just as the robber hopped in his truck. The officers took off after the truck.

The chase was on!

The truck darted in and out of traffic. Officers Torres and Sheldon were close behind. They weren't about to let the suspects escape.

But the suspects weren't about to give up either. They pulled a quick U-turn and headed right for the officers' patrol car!

Officer Torres swerved to the right just in time. Then she turned around and pursued the truck. The high-speed chase continued!

Just then Officer Sheldon radioed for backup. He reported that the suspects were driving down Sunnyslope Avenue. As soon as the other officers arrived, they set up a spike strip. It was time for some teamwork!

RIP! BOOM! BLAM!

The truck went right over the spike strip, causing its front tires to blow out. The driver tried to maintain control, but the car went swirling around and around in circles before crashing into a fire hydrant.

Then the suspects took off on foot!

W 9568

But no one can outrun a police vehicle—especially with Officer Torres behind the wheel!

She cornered the suspects in an alley, and Officer Sheldon leaped out of the car. "Police! Don't move!" he called. "Hands behind your heads!"

The two officers took the suspects into custody, read them their rights, and put them in the back of the police car.

The officers brought the suspects into the police station, booked them, and returned to their patrol car to finish out their shift.

Just then a dog ran right in front of their patrol car!

SCREECH! went the brakes as Officer Torres made a quick stop. "Good thing we were wearing our seat belts!" she said.

The police officers jumped out of their patrol car and approached the dog.

"Be careful," Officer Torres reminded her partner. "You shouldn't touch a strange dog. He might attack." But the dog happily ran over to the officers.

Officer Sheldon found a dog tag on the dog's neck. "Two Gershwin Drive," he read.

"Maybe he was the cause of the accident back on First Street," Officer Torres pointed out. "Let's take him home."

Officer Torres drove to the house listed on the dog's tag. A young boy answered the door.

"You found Follie!" the boy exclaimed. "I thought he was gone forever!"

"This dog needs to be kept on a leash when you take him outside," Officer Sheldon explained.

"Okay, officer," said the boy, as the dog licked his face.

The officers headed back to their patrol car. Their shift was finally over.

"Come on, let's go back to the station," said Officer Torres. "It's been quite a day!" Then she tossed the keys to Officer Sheldon. "I'll even let you drive!" she added with a smile.

EMERGENCY!

By Annie Auerbach

Illustrated by Artful Doodlers

"9-1-1. What is your emergency?" the dispatcher said on the phone. Molly was scared. "Uh, my name is Molly Hunter . . . my mommy fell. She's not getting up!"

"Okay, Molly," the dispatcher said. "We're going to help your mommy. What's your address?"

"146 Pinecone Street," replied Molly.

"I'm sending someone right now," the dispatcher told the girl.

Jane and Simon got the call from dispatch. They were emergency medical technicians, or EMTs. Simon turned on the siren in ambulance number 104 and zoomed down the street. Every second counted.

They arrived at Molly's house and carried in a large medical bag, oxygen, and heart monitor. "Mrs. Hunter?" Jane asked, "Do you know where you are? Where does it hurt?"

Jane began to check Mrs. Hunter's temperature, pulse, and blood pressure.

"Where's Molly?" Mrs. Hunter asked. "My leg hurts."

"Molly is right here, Mrs. Hunter, " Simon said.

"I think we have a slight concussion and possible broken leg," Jane said to Simon. "Let's get her on the stretcher."

"Don't worry, Molly," Jane said, "We'll take good care of your mom."

"Mrs. Hunter, you're going to be okay," Jane said. "But we need to take you to the hospital so they can look at your leg."

Molly stayed with a neighbor while her mother was transported to Hero City Hospital.

Before they left, Molly said to Simon, "Thanks for helping my mommy."

Simon bent down and said to Molly, "You are a very brave little girl. You did the right thing."

Inside the ambulance Jane tended to Mrs. Hunter while Simon drove. He alerted the hospital that they were on their way. Cars moved over to let the ambulance through.

Jane squeezed Mrs. Hunter's hand. "You're going to be just fine," she said.

Mrs. Hunter gave her a grateful smile. "Thank you," she said.

"You're welcome," said Jane as they arrived at the hospital. "We're here to help."

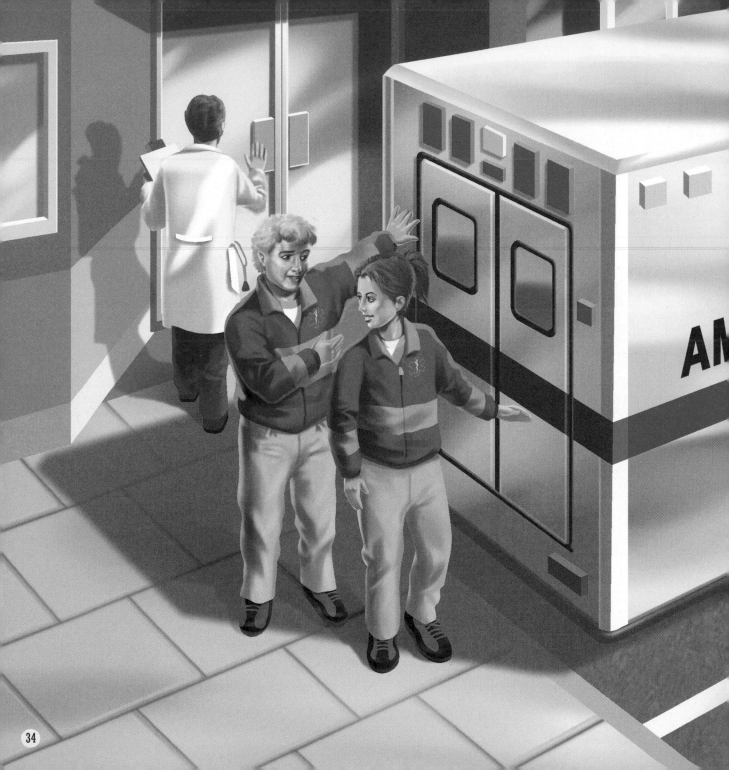

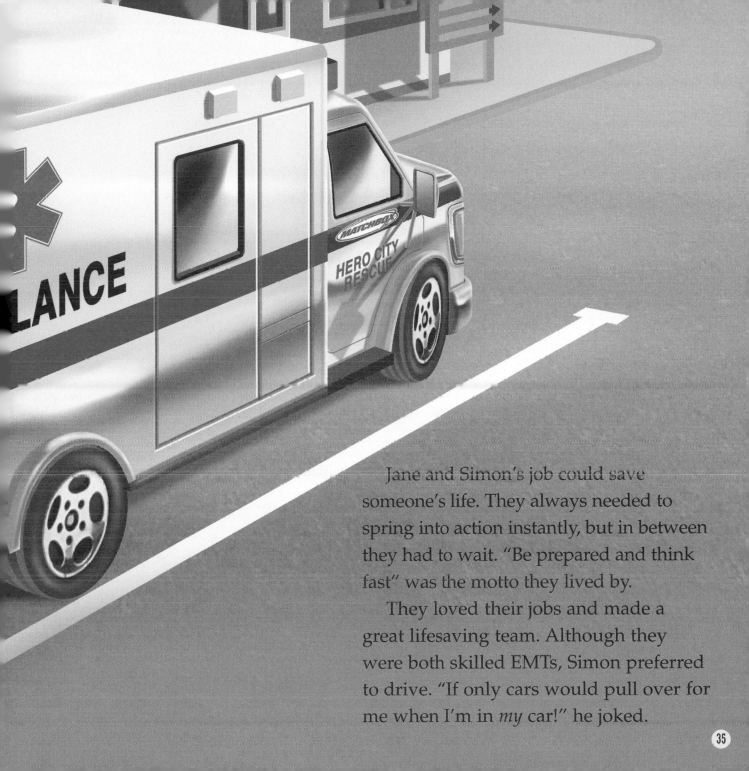

Jane and Simon's job could save someone's life. They always needed to spring into action instantly, but in between they had to wait. "Be prepared and think fast" was the motto they lived by.

They loved their jobs and made a great lifesaving team. Although they were both skilled EMTs, Simon preferred to drive. "If only cars would pull over for me when I'm in *my* car!" he joked.

Just then an emergency call came through from dispatch.
"Dispatch to 104 . . . car pileup on Watson Street near Fourth Avenue."
Simon radioed back, "104 to Dispatch, we're on our way."

Wee-o! Wee-o! The ambulance's siren wailed as the vehicle sped toward the accident site. Even though cars were supposed to pull to the right until the ambulance passed by, Simon had to be extra careful going through intersections. No need for the EMTs to get in an accident too!

Soon the ambulance arrived on the scene. "This looks bad," Jane said. "Let's get to work!"

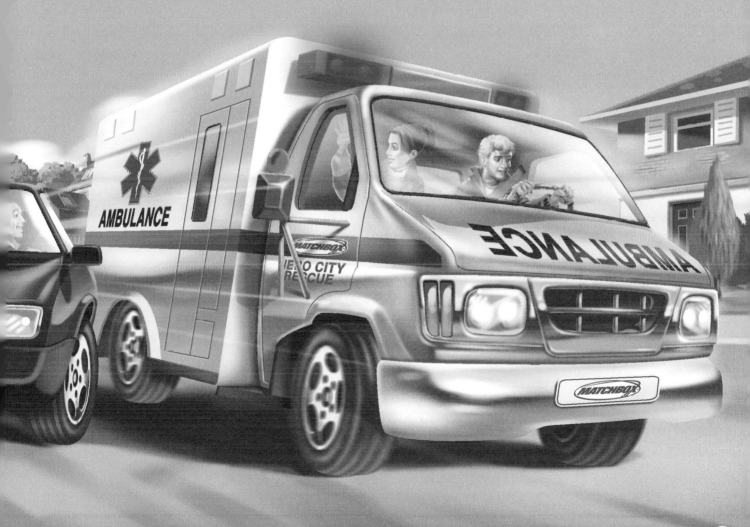

Fire crews, police officers, and EMTs worked together to aid the victims of the multiple vehicle pile-up. Jane tended to a woman who was bleeding, while Simon checked the status of a man who had just been removed from a smashed-up vehicle. The high-speed impact had hurt the man's left knee and arm. He needed to get to a hospital as soon as possible.

But Simon remained calm so as not to alarm the man. "Can you tell me your name, sir?"

"George Webster," the man replied.

Simon said, "Mr. Webster, we're going to take a ride to the hospital."

Jane had finished bandaging up the woman when Simon called her over. "We've got to get him to a hospital—and fast!" he whispered in her ear.

They loaded Mr. Webster into the ambulance, and Jane sat in the back, so she could monitor him.

Simon jumped into the driver's seat and started the engine. But there was one *big* problem. Emergencies had no time schedule and it was rush hour!

Horns blared, brakes screeched, and tempers rose. Rush hour in Hero City was challenging for everyday drivers, but Jane and Simon had to get Mr. Webster to the hospital—fast!

Simon had turned on the siren, but because of the accident the backup of cars was so bad that they couldn't move over to let the ambulance through.

"Boy, I wish this ambulance had wings," Jane called out.

"I know," agreed Simon. "But where there's a will, there's a way—even if it's not the normal way!"

Simon steered the ambulance into the center lane that divided the street. It was a dangerous move, but the ambulance's siren would alert oncoming drivers. As an extra precaution for situations such as this one, the word "ambulance" is spelled backward on the front of the ambulance, so drivers can see it correctly in their rearview mirrors.

While Simon was navigating the roads Jane remained in the back, monitoring Mr. Webster. Suddenly Jane noticed he was having trouble breathing. Jane checked his vitals. She couldn't feel his pulse anymore, and she realized the worst: His heart had stopped beating—and they weren't at the hospital yet!

First Jane performed CPR on him, but it wasn't helping. Luckily an ambulance is a lifesaver on wheels. Everything Jane needed to save Mr. Webster's life is in there. Every second is essential! She grabbed a device called an automatic external defibrillator, or AED, that would send electrical shocks to Mr. Webster's heart so that it would start beating again. But would it work in time?

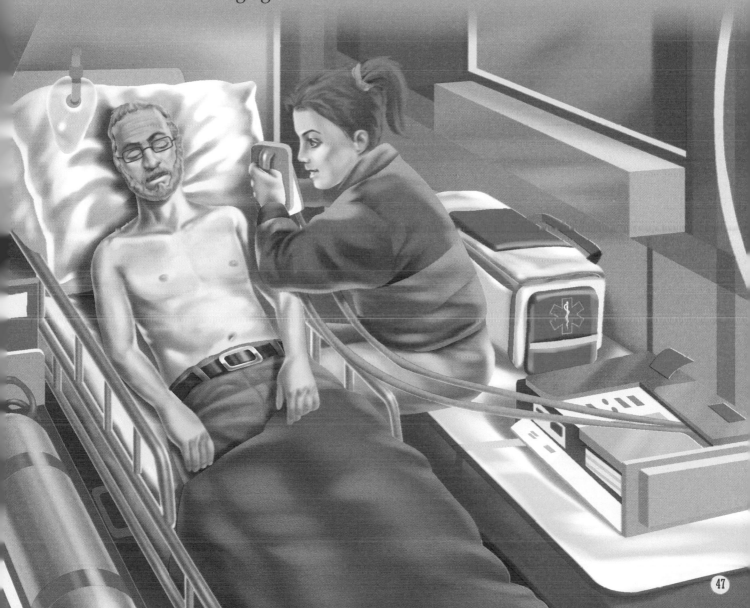

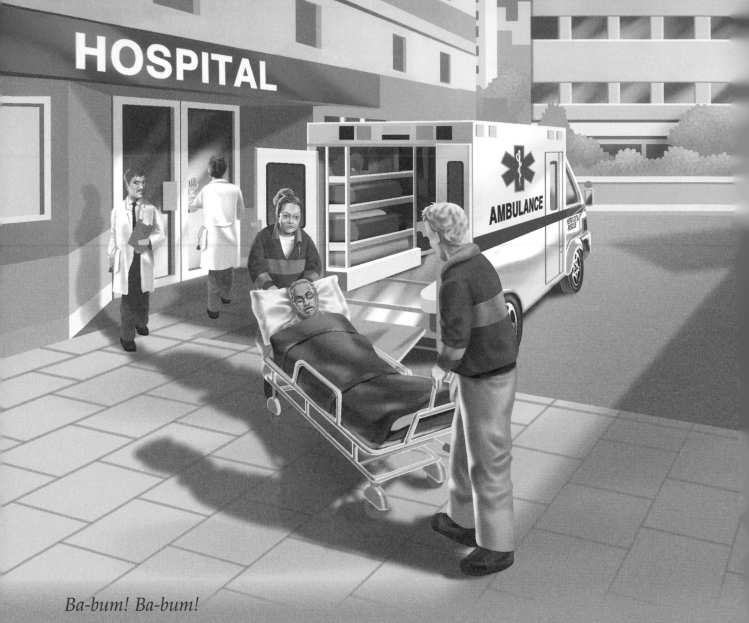

Ba-bum! Ba-bum!

It worked! Mr. Webster's heart was beating normally again! In just a few critical minutes Jane had saved his life.

Once at the hospital Simon leaped out of his seat and helped Jane get Mr. Webster out of the ambulance and into the emergency room.

Leaving the hospital, Simon turned to Jane and said, "Nice work you did!"
Jane smiled. "Yeah, it's been a good day."

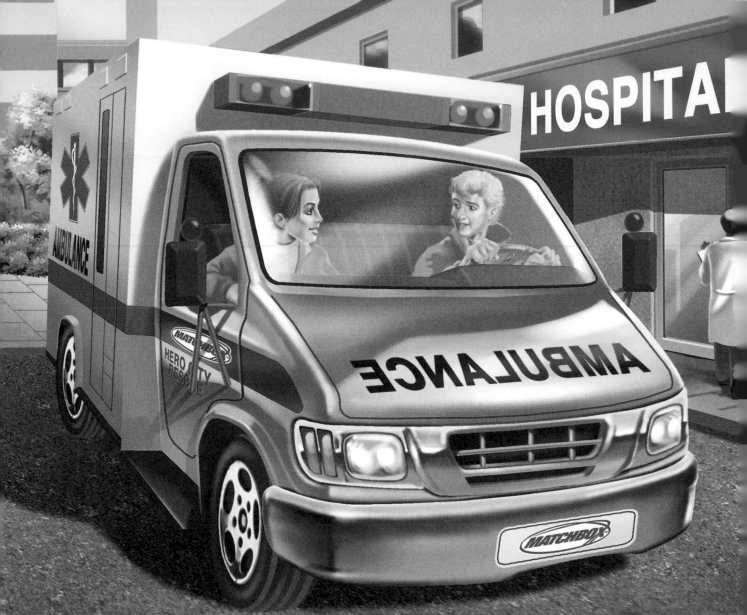

As the pair got back into the ambulance, Jane added, "And nice job on the driving!"

"Just don't tell my son about that little maneuver today!" Simon said with a laugh as they drove off.

Three-Alarm FIRE!

By Annie Auerbach

Illustrated by Joe Ewers and Steve Mitchell

David Donshel arrived at the Hero City fire station at exactly eight A.M. After going through extensive training this was his first day as a firefighter.

"David!" someone called. It was Fred Klein, the fire captain. "Good to have you as part of the team."

"Thank you, sir," David replied. "It's great to be here."

"Come on, I'll introduce you to everyone," said Fred.

David met the other firefighters. The Hero City station had two teams: the engine company, whose truck had water pumps and hoses to put out fires, and the ladder company, which was responsible for search and rescue. David was going to be part of the ladder company.

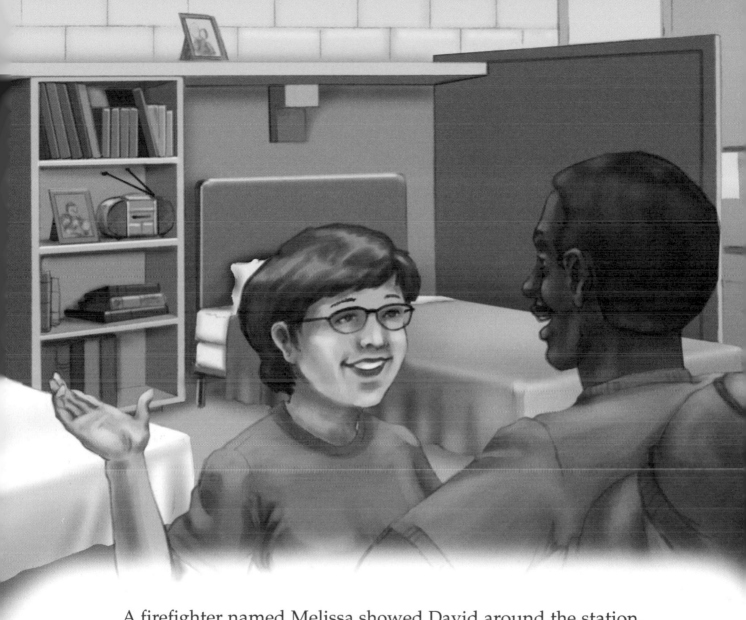

A firefighter named Melissa showed David around the station, including where they ate and slept.

"Welcome to your home away from home," Melissa joked, since firefighters work twenty-four-hour shifts at a time.

David looked around as Adam was inspecting the fire engine. He told David about all of the hoses and pumps on the vehicle. Even though David's specialty was search and rescue, he was still curious about fire engines.

"Hey, don't go trading companies," James teased David. James was a firefighter for the ladder company. He was responsible for maintaining the fire truck.

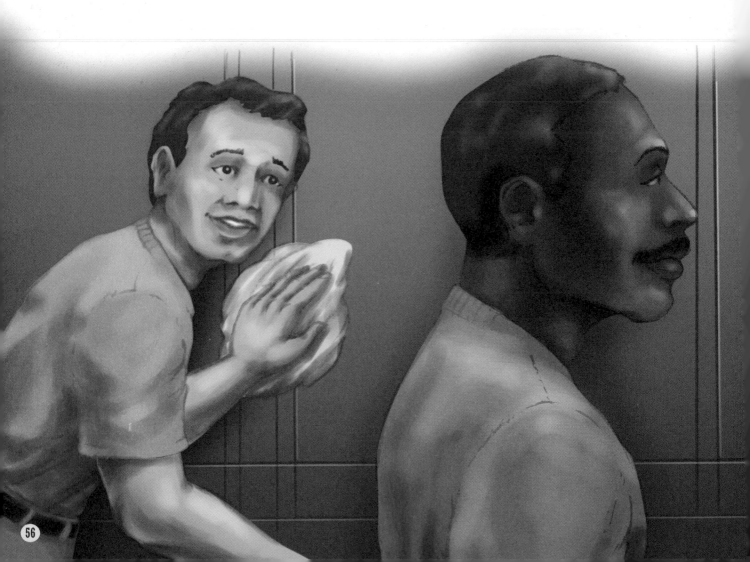

The firefighters had a friendly rivalry. They loved to tease each other.

"Oh, come on," said Adam. "Your ladders are no match for my engine. I have tank that can hold up to one thousand gallons of water!"

"We have more than just ladders," James said proudly. "We have a toolbox on wheels."

Then David jumped into the conversation. "Just remember, Adam: Firefighters don't only put out fires. They also do search and rescue."

James laughed. "That's right! How is that tank of water going to help you then?"

"I know how you can use some water," Fred said. He walked over to the group carrying a bucket and sponge and asked David to wash the ladder truck. "Think of it as your initiation to being part of the team!"

Suddenly the alarm bell rang. The firefighters jumped into action. They hurried to put on their protective gear. Then Fred grabbed the incident report sent by the dispatcher. There was a huge traffic accident on the highway, and a woman was trapped in her car!

It was a job for the ladder company, the experts at search and rescue!

Less than a minute after the alarm bell rang the fire truck pulled out of the station with the siren wailing. Drivers pulled over or stood still as the fire truck went around their cars.

Sitting in the jump seat, David was nervous and excited. It was his first official call!

The fire truck arrived on the scene. A car and a truck had crashed into each other, sending them into the center divider on the freeway. Worst of all, a woman was trapped in her car! The firefighters immediately began their rescue mission.

"Let's try the crowbar," said James.

But it wasn't working. They would have to use a special heavy-duty tool.

David moved at lightning speed. Before long he and James had pried open the roof of the car. The woman trapped inside was eased out. Then Melissa, who was also a medic, examined the woman for any possible injuries.

"Nice job, David," James said afterward. "You worked really quickly."

"Thanks," David replied. "I remember the very first thing I learned in training: 'Every second counts in an emergency!'"

"The number one rule in fire fighting!" agreed James.

That evening David and the other firefighters made dinner at the station since their shift didn't end until the next morning.

"So what do you think of your first day?" James asked David.

"Not bad," replied David. "Although I can't wait to confront my first fire."

"Oh, don't worry," said James. "You'll have plenty of chances!"

James was right. At five-fifteen A.M. the firefighters were woken up by the alarm sounding. Since they slept in their clothes, it only took them a minute to slide down the pole, put on their protective gear, and jump on to their trucks.

Both the engine company and the ladder company were called for this emergency. It was a three-alarm fire!

The sirens blared, and the fire truck and fire engine raced through the streets.

On board each vehicle the firefighters prepared themselves to face the blaze. They put on the tanks and masks that would give them each thirty minutes of air.

At the scene the firefighters saw flames engulfing a four-story house. Without a moment to lose, the firefighters did their tasks. Fred, the fire captain, was in charge of coordinating everyone to put out the fire as quickly and safely as possible. David and the rest of the ladder company raised a ladder up to the roof. Once they were up there, they carefully cut holes in the roof with axes, so trapped smoke could get out.

Meanwhile the engine company unloaded hoses and hooked them up to fire hydrants.

Whoosh!

The water came blasting out of the hoses. There was so much power and pressure that it took two firefighters to hold each hose!

"David, lead the search and rescue team!" Fred ordered and David sprang into action. It was his team's job to make sure no one was still inside the house.

As each firefighter searched a room he put an **X** with chalk on the bottom of the door. This would save essential time.

In the last room David found an elderly man. He swiftly led the man to safety outside the house.

"Melissa!" called David. "I think he's suffering from smoke inhalation."

"I'm on it," she responded and took the man to the waiting ambulance.

But David's job was not over yet! Fred ordered the ladder company to start using the hoses at the top of the building.

"Let's use the aerial ladder," said James. "David, do you want to go up?"

"Sure!" replied David as he climbed into the bucket attached to the end of the ladder.

Eventually the fire was put out—much to the relief of the neighbors.

"Good work, everyone," Fred told the firefighters. And to David, he said, "Welcome to the family."

The tired firefighters made their way back to the station.

Building
HEROES

By Annie Auerbach

Illustrated by S. I. International

At 6:45 Monday morning B. J. was already at the work site. He was meeting with Lisa Gabriel, the architect, to discuss the blueprints. The plan was to tear down an abandoned old building and replace it with a new after-school children's center.

"I'm concerned about the schedule," Lisa said. "We've been delayed a month already because of the weather. What if we don't finish in time?"

B. J. had been a construction manager for fifteen years and had met this type of challenge before. "We'll do our best!" he promised Lisa.

By 7:00 A.M. the heavy-equipment operators had arrived and began to work. B. J. liked to hire people he had worked with before because he knew they were reliable and would do a great job. "We're on a tight deadline, so work quickly, but safely," B. J. told them. "Now let's start tearing down that building."

Crunch! Rip!

The demolition machine tore into the old building. A skilled construction worker named Jack sat in the cab of the demolition machine. By operating a joystick he sent the excavator's gigantic arm into the building.

Once it had grabbed onto a chunk of the building, Jack then mechanically closed the "grabber," pulled back the arm, and then swung the cab around and dumped the contents.

Eventually this powerful machine would demolish the entire building!

Back by the office B. J. and another worker, Sarah, were watching Jack operate the demolition machine in the distance.

"Jack always like to make a mess, doesn't he?" joked B. J.

"Some things never change!" Sarah agreed with a laugh.

"Why don't you operate the loader and clear out some of the rubble?"
B. J. asked.

"Sure thing, boss," Sarah replied.

Sarah slipped a pair of hearing protectors over her ears and climbed into the cab of the front-end loader. Operating the controls, she scooped up the debris in the loader's bucket. She backed up, turned around, and headed toward a dump truck. Then up, up, up the bucket went and—*thump! thump! thump!*—the debris was unloaded. Sarah went back and forth, dumping more debris each time.

The following week B. J. called together all the workers for a meeting. "Everything's going well, but we've got to make up some time," he explained. "How would you all feel about putting in longer hours? If we don't, I'm not sure we'll finish this by September."

The workers exchanged looks. They knew why September was so important—their *own* kids were supposed to go to the after-school center! They all agreed to do whatever it would take to get the job done in time.

Everyone worked extremely hard. They would do long shifts, often trading off who worked nights and who worked days. Huge lights were assembled to help the night workers. Luckily since the building site was in a business district, no residents were affected by the lights or the noise. Although the hours were long, safety and quality were still top priorities. B. J. made certain of that.

By November the old building was gone, and the debris cleared. The new building would need a strong foundation of steel rods and concrete, so first a very large hole had to be dug in the ground. It was a perfect job for an excavator.

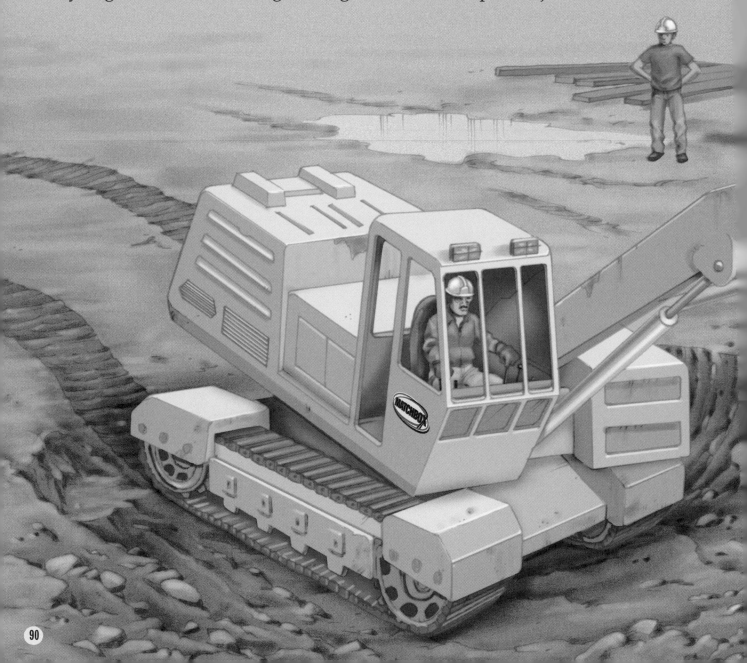

Once again Jack climbed into the cab and got to work. He used the controls so that the machine would scoop up a large load of dirt and gravel, swing around, and drop the contents into a dump truck nearby.

As soon as the dump truck was full of dirt and gravel, it was Tony's job to transport it to an off-site location. When he got there the back of the dump truck was tipped up and the contents were dumped out. Then it was back to the work site to fill up again!

Finally the huge hole was completely dug up, and Luis Alvarez and his cement mixer were called in. This vehicle had a special feature: To keep the cement from getting hard, it would constantly turn within the truck itself. Luis called it his "churn-and-turn machine."

Once the cement was sent from the truck on the conveyer, it was poured around steel rods. Together this would make the foundation safe.

Building the after-school center was strenuous work, but the machines helped the workers out tremendously. They could lift, dump, churn, and mechanically do things that saved a lot of time and strength.

But would it be enough to finish the after-school center in time?

The hard work paid off, and the day before school started, there was a grand opening and ribbon-cutting ceremony for the new center.

Everyone was proud of the construction workers—especially their own children.

B. J. thanked each of the workers individually. "I couldn't have done it without you," he told them.

And the workers couldn't have done it without the very large heroes: the construction vehicles!